First Time

Going to a Concert

Melinda Beth Radabaugh

Heinemann Library

Chicago, Illinois

Customer Service 888-454-2279
Visit our website at www.heinemannlibrary.com

Designed by Sue Emerson, Heinemann Library; Page layout by Que-Net Media™
Printed and bound in the United States by Lake Book Manufacturing, Inc.
Photo research by Janet Lankford-Moran

08 07 06 05 04
10 9 8 7 6 5 4 3 2 1

Library of Congress Cataloging-in-Publication Data
Radabaugh, Melinda Beth.
  Going to a concert / Melinda Beth Radabaugh.
      v. cm. – (First time)
Includes index.
Contents: What is a concert? – What kinds of concerts are there? – Where is a concert held? – Who will be at a concert? – What happens when you go to a concert? – What will happen during the concert? – What will the performers use? – What will the performers wear? – What happens when the concert is over?
  ISBN 1-4034-3867-6 (HC), 1-4034-3882-X (Pbk.)
  1. Concerts–Social aspects–Juvenile literature. 2. Music–Performance–Social aspects–Juvenile literature. [1. Concerts. 2. Music–Performance.] I. Title. II. Series.
  ML3928.R23 2003

                                        2002155330

Acknowledgments
The author and publishers are grateful to the following for permission to reproduce copyright material:
p. 4 Philip Gould/Corbis; pp. 5, 10, 12, 13, 14, 15, 20, 21 Robert Lifson/Heinemann Library; p. 6 Frank Siteman/Mira.com; pp. 7, 8, 9 Stone/Getty Images; p. 11 Mauritius/Index Stock Imagery, Inc.; pp. 16, 17 The Image Bank/Getty Images; p. 18 Eric Roth/Index Stock Imagery, Inc.; p. 19 Guy Cali/Stock Connection/PictureQuest; p. 22 (row 1, L-R) PhotoDisc, Corbis; (row 2, L-R) PhotoDisc, Robert Lifson/Heinemann Library; (row 3, L-R) PhotoDisc, Corbis; p. 23 (row 1, L-R) Stone/Getty Images, PhotoDisc, PhotoDisc, Dennis Degnan/Corbis; (row 2, L-R) Corbis, PhotoDisc, Corbis, Guy Cali/Stock Connection/PictureQuest; (row 3, L-R) Robert Lifson/Heinemann Library, PhotoDisc, Robert Lifson/Heinemann Library, Stone/Getty Images; (row 4) Robert Lifson/Heinemann Library; p. 24 (column 1) PhotoDisc; (column 2, T-B) PhotoDisc, Robert Lifson/Heinemann Library; back cover Robert Lifson/Heinemann Library

Cover photograph by Robert Lifson/Heinemann Library

Special thanks to our advisory panel for their help in the preparation of this book:

Alice Bethke, Library Consultant
Palo Alto, CA

Eileen Day, Preschool Teacher
Chicago, IL

Kathleen Gilbert,
Second Grade Teacher
Round Rock, TX

Sandra Gilbert,
Library Media Specialist
Fiest Elementary School
Houston, TX

Jan Gobeille,
Kindergarten Teacher
Garfield Elementary
Oakland, CA

Angela Leeper,
Educational Consultant
Wake Forest, NC

Some words are shown in bold, **like this.**
You can find them in the picture glossary on page 23.

Contents

What Is a Concert?

performer

A concert is a special show.

Performers sing, dance, or play music on the **stage**.

You watch and listen to the performers.

You sit in the **audience.**

What Kinds of Concerts Are There?

There are music concerts.

There are dance concerts, too.

Some concerts are for children.

Other concerts are for grown-ups.

Where Are Concerts Held?

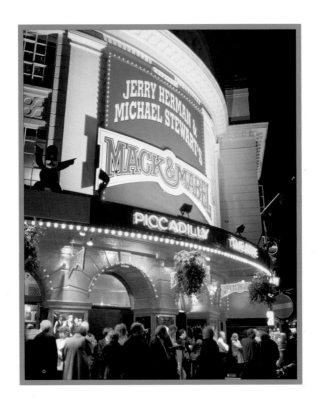

Concerts are usually in a **theater**.

A theater has lots of seats inside.

Some concerts can be outdoors.

Others are at a school.

Who Will You See at a Concert?

You will see people in the **audience**.

An **usher** will help you find your seat.

You will see **musicians** playing music.

You may see **dancers** and singers, too.

What Happens When You Go to a Concert?

First, you buy a **ticket**.

Next, you show your ticket to an **usher**.

Then, you get a **program.**

It tells you about the concert.

What Will Happen During the Concert?

curtain

You wait for the lights to go out.

Then, the **curtain** opens.

Then, the concert begins!

You clap when a song is over.

What Will the Performers Use?

instrument

Musicians play **instruments**.

There are many different kinds of instruments.

Musicians read **sheet music** to play the songs.

The sheet music rests on **music stands.**

What Will the Performers Wear?

The **musicians** may wear
fancy clothes.

Sometimes **performers** wear **costumes.**

Costumes can help tell a story.

What Happens When the Concert Is Over?

At the end the **performers** take a bow.

You clap your hands.

The **curtain** closes and the lights come on.

Time to go home!

Quiz

What can you find at a concert?

Look for the answer on page 24.

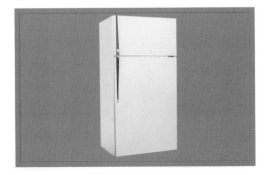

Picture Glossary

audience
pages 5, 10

instrument
page 16

program
page 13

theater
page 8

costume
page 19

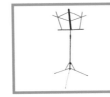

music stand
page 17

sheet music
page 17

ticket
page 12

curtain
pages 14, 21

musician
pages 11, 16, 17, 18

stage
page 4

usher
pages 10, 12

dancer
page 11

performer
pages 4, 5, 19, 20

Note to Parents and Teachers

Reading for information is an important part of a child's literacy development. Learning begins with a question about something. Help children think of themselves as investigators and researchers by encouraging their questions about the world around them. Each chapter in this book begins with a question. Read the question together. Look at the pictures. Talk about what you think the answer might be. Then read the text to find out if your predictions were correct. Think of other questions you could ask about the topic, and discuss where you might find the answers. Assist children in using the picture glossary and the index to practice new vocabulary and research skills.

Index

Answer to quiz on page 22

You can find the instrument, the ticket, and the sheet music at a concert.